CIRCLE OF JUSTICE

ADITYA SHARMA

Made with ♥ on the Notion Press Platform
www.notionpress.com

Contents

1

"Dude, where the fuck are you?"

Huffing, I slammed my hand down on the kitchen counter, wishing like hell I could throw my cell against the wall and never talk to anyone again. "On my way," I growled.

Cliff sighed. "What's taking so long?"

If he only knew. It was a bad day for me. Hell, every fucking day was worse than the last. It didn't help that my father liked to call and remind me of my failure every goddamn week. "I'll be there in a minute," I snapped.

"Dude, hurry up. Emma's been asking about you. I think tonight's gonna be your night, if you get out of your shitty mood."

I hung up the phone and took a deep breath, my fists clenched tight to keep my hands from shaking. Sometimes I wished my friends knew about my past, so I wouldn't have to come up with bullshit excuses every time I got pissed. Cliff was my friend and we started up a band a couple of years ago, but he didn't know about my real life; neither did Emma.

When I picked up and moved from Charleston to attend college in the North Carolina Mountains, I'd left everything behind. None of the students recognized me, or put together the pieces of who I actually was. It was nice for a while, but

I was living a lie. I fought the urges inside of me every single day.

Hurrying out of my apartment, I took the stairs two at a time. The smell of weed wafted past my nose. I'd give anything to smoke a blunt and forget life for a while, but it wouldn't help. I could be stoned off my ass, or in bed with random college chicks, and still not be able to forget.

The night air was so cold I pulled my hoodie over my head and started on my way through the parking lot to one of the back street shortcuts. Snow had begun to fall and by the end of the night, the ground would be covered. Since I planned on getting drunk and going home with Emma, I didn't see the need in driving my truck.

Emma Turner was one of the only girls on campus I hadn't tried to fuck. She was more to me than just some friend, or singer in my band. However, tonight I didn't give a shit. If she wanted me, I was damn well going to make sure she got it. To hell with the consequences.

The wind whipped by my ear, howling so hard it sounded like a scream. The street wasn't lit, but that didn't bother me. I liked it that way. The bar was only a quarter of a mile away, so I hoped the silence would help my mood. The last thing I wanted was to be a dick to Emma when she didn't deserve it.

Another muffled sound caught my attention and I stopped. There were school apartments to my right, music blaring from one of the many parties going on. However, this sound had come from my left, the direction of the woods. I heard it again and my body froze. It was a woman's scream. Only someone within close distance would've heard it.

What made my blood boil were the sounds that followed. It was as if everything inside of me snapped. The urges I'd fought for so long surfaced—there was no going back. Taking off into the woods, I was nearly blinded by my rage. The sounds grew louder and it sickened me to the core.

Everything was dark, but it wasn't enough to hide what was going on. The girl's face was pushed into the ground to muffle her screams while the fucker undid his pants, her skirt lifted and underwear ripped. She fought as hard as she could, but she was no match for his size.

I needed him to suffer . . . but even more than that, I wanted him dead. Without a word, I closed the distance and grabbed him around the neck. Hauling him up, I slammed him against a tree. It felt good to hear his howls of pain.

"What the fuck?" he spat, reeking of beer.

Squeezing his neck, I bashed him against the tree, his eyes growing wide in terror. "Feel like a man now?" I growled. "It's not so fun when you're helpless, is it?"

He gasped for air. "She . . . wanted . . . it."

Teeth clenched, I squeezed harder. "You're a pathetic son of a bitch. Let me guess, she wanted it as badly as you want this." I dropped him down, long enough to grab his chin and the back of his head. Snapping his neck, I watched him collapse lifeless to the ground.

The moment stilled my breath. I hadn't known what it would feel like to kill someone, to know it was me who took their life. Out of all the emotions I could have guessed I'd experience, pure elation wouldn't have been one of them. The high that buzzed through my body felt like nothing I'd ever experienced before. There was no remorse, no guilt for what I'd done. He deserved to die, like the countless other men out there who preyed on innocent women.

The girl's whimpers brought me back. With my hood over my head, I turned to face her. Knowing I was backlit by the moon, she couldn't see my face through her tears and the dark. Her shirt was torn and she scrambled to lower her skirt.

"You're safe now," I said, helping her up by the hand. Her whole body shook and she fell into my arms, her cries echoing in my ear. I had to get away. "You need to get help. Run to the apartments and call 911. Now!"

I let her go and she took off out of the woods toward the apartments, while I raced back to mine. There was only one thing I could do. Once I was in my apartment, I grabbed the phone out of my pocket and found my father's number. He picked up by the end of the first ring.

"What's wrong, son?"

I leaned against the door, knowing my life was about to get exponentially more fucked up. "I'm ready. Just tell me what I have to do."

"Summer's coming. It's getting warmer every day," Linda said, setting down my plate of eggs and bacon. She was in her late sixties, with short, white hair. I don't think there was ever a morning where she didn't wear something pink.

I took a sip of my coffee. "That it is. Luckily, I don't plan on staying in town for much longer." For the past two months, I'd eaten breakfast at her and her husband's diner every morning. Boston was just one of the cities on my list. It was time to move on.

Her brows furrowed. "You moving?"

I nodded. "New York. Lots of people over there I want to . . . see."

Frowning, she filled up my coffee cup. "I hate to see you go, young man. I'm going to miss seeing you in here every morning. Make sure to stop in again if you're ever in town."

"I will."

Once she was gone, I turned my attention to the window. The second I heard the sirens, I grinned. Others in the diner rushed to the windows, jockeying for position to see what was going on. I knew it was only a matter of time before they found his body.

The crowd grew thick with onlookers, especially when the media showed up. Linda turned on the TV so we could hear the live coverage. "Another Trigger victim . . ." That was one of the names they called me, Trigger. The others were: serial killer, murderer, vigilante, and the list went on and on. I didn't give a fuck what the people thought. I did what I had to do.

I finished my breakfast and walked up to the counter. Linda's husband came out from the kitchen and stood beside her, both of their eyes fixed on the TV. "I bet it's that serial killer again," she stated. "It's making me nervous."

Roger put his arm around her. "I'll protect you, sweetheart."

Pulling out my wallet, I placed my money on the counter. "From what I understand, the victims are all criminals. I think you'll be fine."

Linda looked at me and sighed. "He's still a killer. Only God is allowed to dole out that kind of punishment."

"True, but not everyone wants to wait for an eternity." I slid the money over to her. "Be safe out there." I walked out of the restaurant and down the street to my car. My bags were packed and I had my rifle secured in the trunk. New York was going to keep me busy for a while.

My phone rang as soon as I got onto the highway. The caller's name popped up on my dashboard, and I blew out a frustrated breath as I pressed the button to accept it. "Hello, Glenn."

Glenn Chandler was my superior and also a good friend of my father's. They'd worked together for years in the Coast Guard, until Glenn branched out and not only joined a secret group headed by the FBI, but built a multi-billion-dollar company as well. We were fully trained, lethal assassins. I never knew anything like that existed, until my father wanted me to join. I'd spent the past eight years training and working for the FBI.

“Would you like to explain what the fuck you’re doing up there?” Glenn demanded.

“I’m heading to New York. My time in Boston’s done.”

“You’re damn right it is. What the hell were you thinking? You can’t keep doing this, son. If you get caught, my superiors will be up my ass even more so than they are right now. They want you to slow down.”

Releasing a heavy sigh, I sat back in my seat. “It had to be done.”

“Not like that it didn’t. We have to be careful. A kill here and there is fine, but every day? It’s too much. I want to kill the bastards as much as you do, but we can’t risk exposing what we are. If you can’t follow the rules, you’re out.”

I couldn’t afford to be kicked out. I needed the group. Killing was an addiction I couldn’t let go. It was all I had left. “I need this, Glenn. You know that.”

He blew out a shaky breath. “I know, son. But I don’t want to see you go down the same path your father did.”

And there it was . . . the one thing I didn’t want to hear. I hadn’t seen my father in years. Not since he got drunk and wrapped his car around a telephone pole, paralyzing himself. Now he was a resident of Green Meadows, an assisted living facility.

“I’m not that stupid,” I snarled.

“Now don’t start that shit. You don’t know how hard it was for him when your mother and sister were murdered. He blamed himself for not being there.”

“Bullshit. He blamed me. It was my fault we weren’t there to protect them. Why else do you think he tried to recruit me when I turned eighteen? He thought it was my duty.” I’d been the one who wanted to go on that fishing trip. If it wasn’t for us leaving home, they’d still be alive. That was why I left Charleston, to get away from it all.

"He wanted your support, Preston. The desire to find the man who killed your family was too much on him."

"And look where that got us. It's been thirteen years and we still don't know who the fucker is."

The line went quiet, before Glenn sighed. "I need you in Charleston."

"Fuck that. I'm going to New York."

"It's an order, Hale. Either you come down to Charleston, or I'll have my sons hunt you down. You know very well they'll find you."

"Fuck," I growled, slamming my hand on the steering wheel so hard the pain shot up my arm. "What the hell are you even doing down there?" Glenn's multi-billion-dollar company was in Charlotte, North Carolina. There was no reason for him to be in Charleston, other than to see my father.

"I'm here visiting your father. It's time you saw him too." I knew it. "But there's something else . . ."

"What's that?" I grumbled. The exit to New York City drew closer, but instead of taking it, I continued south on Interstate 95. I couldn't believe I was doing this shit.

"Your mother and sister's case is going to be reopened," he informed me.

It was as if everything around me came to a halt. Swerving to the side of the road, I slammed on the brakes, tires screeching. "What happened?" For them to reopen the case after so many years, they had to have new evidence.

Glenn cleared his throat. "There was a murder last night. I wanted to catch you before you saw it on the news."

"Go on," I snapped. My whole body shook, my hands aching to hold the cold metal of a gun between them.

"Judging by the details, I think he's the one."

Heart racing, I could feel the rage coursing through my body. Stepping on the gas, I hurled back onto the interstate. "On my way."

3

Closing my eyes, I breathed in the salty sea air and smiled, propping my feet up on the wrought iron rails of the balcony connected to my room. I loved the way the waves sounded as they crashed along the shore. We'd been in Charleston for the past week, staying at one of Glenn's many homes. And I hadn't had to do a single thing other than relax, which was odd. Working for one of the richest men on the east coast had its perks, but he was interesting to say the least. I'd been under his employ for a little over eight months now.

A knock sounded on the bedroom door. Opening my eyes, I sat up straighter and turned toward the sound. "Come in," I called.

The door opened and Glenn stepped inside, his face a stony mask. I'd seen that look a million times, but could never decipher what it meant. His dark hair had more wisps of gray than it did when he'd hired me.

"Are you busy?" he asked.

I jumped out of my seat, setting my notebook on the deck table. "Of course not. Is there something I can do for you?"

He shook his head. "Not at the moment. I wanted to stop by and share our plans." He walked further into my room and looked out toward the ocean, his crisp, button-down shirt and pants perfectly pressed. I'd never seen him look normal, in something as mundane as a pair of jeans and a T-shirt. "I'm sorry for being scarce the past week. Something came up that required my attention," he said, turning his attention to me.

"No worries. I was just working on a new song."

His lip pulled into a small smile, a rare occurrence. "How's it coming along?"

I shrugged. "Okay, I guess. It's been so long since I've written one. It'll probably sound horrible."

"I very much doubt that," he added. "I've heard you sing some of your songs under your breath." Blood rushed to my face in embarrassment. "But one of the things I wanted to talk to you about is my son," he continued. "How would you feel about working for him when I retire?"

My pulse spiked and I could feel my heart pound. Wade Chandler was twenty-nine, just two years older than me, but he made me nervous. He was extremely good looking, yet serious all the time, hardly ever smiling. I'd seen so many people give into him from a single stare. Even though I'd worked for Chandler Enterprises for several months, I'd only spoken to Wade maybe three times, and that was a 'how are you doing' type of thing.

Brows furrowed, Glenn stared at me. "Is something wrong?"

"No," I blurted with a laugh. "Are you sure he'd want to work with me? We've never really spoken to each other."

He nodded. "I know, but it was his idea to take you on. I thought I'd ask first, to see if you were interested. The money would be the same. He thought you two could get to know each other better when he arrives."

"Is he coming to Charleston?"

Glenn's phone rang and he looked down at the screen before shutting off the sound. "He'll be here tomorrow morning," he said, lifting his gaze to mine.

"All right, I can do it," I answered. "I'm always up for a challenge."

He smiled. "You'll do fine. Once he gets to know you, he won't be so . . . uptight."

"Glad to hear it."

He started to take a step back and stopped. "There's something else I wanted to tell you. I'm hosting a dinner tomorrow night and I need you to be here. Wade will be joining us, but I have another guest who'll be arriving in town later tonight as well."

"Okay," I said with a nod. "Is there anything you need me to plan for the dinner?"

He shook his head and walked to the door. "Mrs. Walker has it handled. I do, however, need you to find a nice dress to wear. You can charge it to the company card. The Mercedes is in the garage if you want to take it." He paused at the door and glanced at me over his shoulder. "Oh, and I won't be around this evening, but Mrs. Walker will cook your dinner when you're ready."

"Thank you." I waved as he walked out the door and shut it behind him.

It wasn't the first time I had to buy an evening gown for one of his formal events, or even drive one of his expensive cars. My biggest fear was wrecking one of them, but he didn't seem to care. Fifty thousand dollars to him was like pocket change. My family hadn't had a lot of money when I was growing up, so it was strange experiencing how the other half lived.

Working for Chandler Enterprises wasn't exactly what I thought I'd do with my college degree. After graduating with a BA in creative writing, I'd moved back to Charlotte and held a job at the local newspaper. I'd done that for five years, until out of nowhere, the infamous Glenn Chandler approached me as I walked out of the office one day. He offered me three times as much to work as his assistant and write his business proposals. I couldn't pass it up.

Grabbing my brush, I ran it through my long, blonde hair before pulling it into a ponytail. It was time to shop for my dress. Mrs. Walker was in the kitchen cleaning off the counters when I entered. She was a middle-aged woman with shoulder-length, brown hair and a kind smile. Since Glenn hadn't needed my assistance as of late, I'd been helping her in the kitchen from time to time.

"Do you need anything while I'm out?" I asked her.

She looked over at me and smiled, tossing her dishrag in the sink. "No, I'm good, sweetheart. I went to the grocery store this morning."

"Okay. I'll be back this afternoon and I can help you with dinner. We should eat together, since Glenn will be gone."

Her face brightened. "I'd like that. My husband has to work late anyway. We can eat out on the terrace."

"I look forward to it." I waved goodbye and walked into the garage, where the sleek, black Mercedes sat. I cranked it up and started on my way to downtown Charleston. King Street was the place to go, so I parked in one of the first places I could find and hopped out of the car. Before I could even shut the door, my phone rang.

"Hey, Mom," I answered.

"Hey, baby. How are you?"

Shutting the car door, I locked it and hurried across the street. "Good. Just out trying to find a dress for a dinner tomorrow night."

"That sounds nice. You still liking your job?"

I laughed. "Can't complain. I'm making more money than I would anywhere else. Besides, I've basically had the whole week off, with pay. It's nice to sit on the beach and write." My mom cleared her throat nervously. "What is it?"

"You aren't—you're not sleeping with him are you?" she asked, her voice low.

I burst out laughing. "Oh my God, I can't believe you asked that. No, I'm not sleeping with him. Eww . . . he's like a father figure to me. It's not like that, I promise."

"Okay, just making sure. It's been weighing on my mind for a while now."

"You have nothing to worry about. However, when he retires, I'll be working for his son. Now that will be interesting."

"Oh," she said, drawing out the word. "Yes, it will. He's an attractive man."

"With zero personality. Trust me, there'll be no mixing business with pleasure. He's coming down to Charleston tomorrow. Glenn wants us to get to know each other, since we'll be working together in the near future."

"Just be careful. The Chandler men strike me as the kind of guys who get what they want. Don't let them run all over you."

I shook my head and smiled. Glenn and Wade had always treated me with respect. "I won't, Momma. Is that all you called to say?"

She sighed. "No, it's not. I wanted to tell you to be careful down there."

"What do you mean?"

"I was walking by the break room and saw the news. A lot of the nurses were talking about a young woman around your age who was found murdered on the beach. As of right now, they don't have any leads, which means the killer's still out there. Don't go walking around at night by yourself."

Chills ran up my spine. "Did they say where she was found, or how she was killed?" I loved walking on the beach at night.

"They haven't announced the details, but she was found not far from where you're staying. I just want you to be safe."

"I will, Mom. I'm almost always with Glenn, so nobody's going to get to me."

"All right, baby. I love you. Make sure to call your father when you get a chance. You know how he likes to hear from you when you're away."

We said our goodbyes and I walked into the boutique. My safe haven no longer felt safe.

What the hell was I doing back in Charleston? It was a huge goddamn mistake. If Glenn wanted to wrangle me in, he'd fucked up. If anything, being back made everything worse. I had no intention of facing my father, not until the man who screwed up our lives was dead. All I wanted was for the guilt to go away. No matter how many rapists and child molesters I killed, nothing worked.

My sister, Cameron, had been killed by strangulation just outside of our house on the beach, while my mother died inside. There was a struggle, but she tried her best to protect my sister, only to die from a blunt head trauma. If my father and I had been home, there's a chance they could've survived. Instead, they died alone and afraid. The thought sickened me to the core.

Glenn was parked in the Sea Dunes motel parking lot, his stare never wavering from mine when I pulled in beside him. He waved me over, so I got out of my car and joined him in the backseat while his driver stood outside. It'd been almost a year since I'd seen him last.

"You look terrible," he said, pursing his lips.

"I'm sure you would too if you drove all fucking day without stopping," I snapped.

"That's why you're going to stay at my house while you're in town. The pool house is all ready for you. And once we're done in Charleston, you're going to work for me in Charlotte. It's about time you do something with your life besides killing people."

I was about to blast off, but he held up his hand.

"Don't even think about arguing with me. I know you don't want to be here, but there's no other choice. You're the only one who can help."

I huffed. "How's that? I haven't been in this town for years."

"You're right. But I'm hoping after you see this, it'll spark your interest." There was a folder in the seat pocket in front of him. He pulled it out and handed it to me. "Grady McConnell, the chief of police here, gave me this today. He's at the scene now waiting for us. He's going to let us look around."

Bile rose up the back of my throat. Flashbacks of seeing my mother and Cameron's bodies ran rampant through my mind. I'd looked at their files a thousand times, hoping to figure out the puzzle. I didn't want this to be the same way.

The last thing I expected was to know who the victim was.

"Fuck," I hissed, staring at a picture of the bright-eyed girl I once sat beside in my high school class. Shelly Price was one of the smart ones, always concentrating on her school work. Unlike me, who cared more about sports than anything else.

From the crime scene photos, she was strangled to death . . . just like Cameron. There were no other marks on her body, except for her neck.

According to the report, she'd been raped, but it wasn't until after she died. Sick fucker. I slammed the file shut and closed my eyes, clenching my teeth so hard the muscles in my jaw hurt. "Why didn't you tell me who it was?" I growled, trying to slow my breathing.

Glenn's voice lowered, but I could tell he was ready to grab me if I lost control. "I thought if you found out, it'd set you off and I'd have to hunt you down. If this is the same guy who murdered your sister, then she's the key. I need you to dig deeper."

"How?"

His gaze softened. "You need to go home, Preston. Search that house until you've combed every square inch. Something's been missed and it needs to be found."

The car felt smaller by the minute. I had to get the fuck out of there. "Forget it."

Jerking the door open, I stormed outside and slammed it shut. There was no way in hell I was going back to my childhood home. I had no clue what the place even looked like now that my father didn't live there anymore. It was probably falling apart.

The wind had picked up and the rotten decay of death surrounded me. Everywhere I went, it was all around me. Across the street, the waves crashed on the beach and there was a glow of lights where the police were investigating the scene of the crime. I wasn't the police, just a killer who worked for the FBI. I doled out punishment—just the way I liked it.

A door slammed behind me and Glenn's footsteps approached. "This could be your chance to end this, son. I know there's more to you than mindless killing. Open yourself up. Use that potential your father always told me about." His arm brushed against mine as we stared out at the dark, crashing waters. "He misses you, Preston."

"Does he know about Shelly?"

An audible sigh escaped his lips. "Yes. When he found out, he was chomping at the bit to help."

I could only imagine the pain and anger he must be feeling. I'd have killed myself if I was stuck in a wheelchair for the rest of my life.

Glenn placed a hand on my shoulder. "If he knows you're here and that you're helping, it'll make a world of difference. He'll feel like he's a part of it."

"I can't. Not yet."

"It's your choice. I'm sure you'll make the right decision." He patted my shoulder and started across the road. "Now come on."

I followed him to where the crime scene was marked off with yellow tape. The only way to get through this mess was to shut myself off. But that'd be easy. I'd done it so much, I didn't even know who I was anymore.

#

Every time I closed my eyes to sleep, I saw visions of the people my targets had tortured. The smiling faces of kids who would never know what it was like to be innocent again, or the women who would always be looking over their shoulders for the next attacker. It was an endless dream I couldn't control. The only time it got better was when I killed.

Drenched in sweat, I glanced over at the bedside clock. It was three in the fucking morning. Even being in Glenn's pool house, with probably the most comfortable bed I'd ever sat on, going back to sleep would still be impossible. Unless . . .

My computer bag sat on the floor, beckoning me to open it. It was like a beacon, silently telling me it was time. It was the longest I'd ever gone without finding a target.

"Fuck it," I grumbled low.

Grabbing a clean black shirt from my bag, I put it on and reached for my computer. I turned on my laptop and felt the adrenaline coursing through my veins. There was a special government software only my group had access to. It gave us the names and addresses of possible targets, including their everyday activities. We could see which ones were eliminated and by who. Wade Chandler, Glenn's oldest son, and I were neck and neck on most kills, but I had him beat by two. Well, three, after tonight.

Scrolling down the list, my whole body shook in anticipation. It shouldn't make someone happy to kill another being, but I craved it. Grinning wide, I found a target in North Charleston. Jim Butler was right up my alley. He'd served time in prison for raping his step-daughter, damaging her so bad she wouldn't be able to have children when she got older. Most of the time, men like that didn't survive prison, but the fucker must've had luck on his side. He sure as hell wasn't going to survive me.

Grabbing my gun, I holstered it at my hip, pocketing two extra magazines for good measure. Glenn better not even think about trying to stop me. Taking my car keys, I clutched them in my hand and stormed out of the pool house. There were no lights on in the main house, but as soon as I walked past the pool, a light blared to life.

I turned to face the window, only to find Glenn staring at me. We faced off. I dared him to come out and stop me. Instead, he turned his head and shut off the light. He thought I needed to be saved, but I didn't need saving.

#

Jim's house was pitch black, and there was an old, beat-up truck in the driveway. Slipping around to the back of the house, I pried open the lock to the patio door and crept inside. Everything smelled like garbage and piss. The fucker snored so loud it led me right to his bedroom. He was by himself, sleeping on his back, with a hand behind his head as if he hadn't a care in the world.

I kicked his bed and he jerked awake, his hands wiping at his face. "Wha—what's going on?"

"Rise and shine, cocksucker. That must be how you stayed alive in prison . . . sucking dick."

"Who are you?" he shouted, scrambling off the bed and backing against the wall. Only, he didn't get far enough.

I pointed my gun straight at his cock and fired. His screams were deafening, and all I could do was smile as he flailed around on the floor, bleeding from his groin. He scrambled and clawed himself to the corner of the room, his face a mask of sheer terror.

Good. I wanted him to feel fear, to know what it was like to be terrified. No amount of torture was going to take away what he did. But at least his victims would know he died a horrible death. His step-daughter was the only one documented, but men like him had to hurt others; it was what they lived for.

Butler looked up at me as I towered over him, pointing my gun at his head. "Please," he begged, his body shaking.

Hearing that word infuriated the fuck out of me. There was no room for mercy. He didn't deserve it. Finger on the trigger, I glared down at him. "This is for Milly."

5

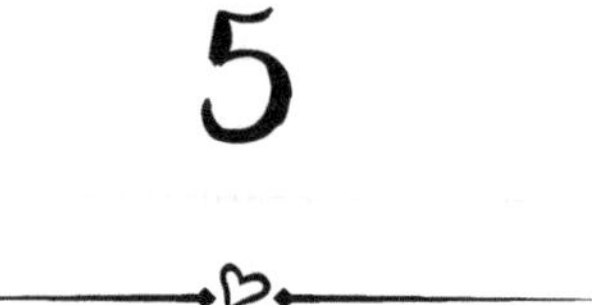

Glenn didn't need me again this morning, so I grabbed my notepad and walked across the street to White Point Garden. Just last night, I'd watched a couple get married in the white gazebo in the middle of the park. It made me realize that was never going to be me. I didn't have time for men, other than Glenn and my father.

I walked up to the gazebo and sat down, enjoying the breeze. Summer was already here, and once July came, it'd be so hot you could barely breathe. Although, it'd definitely be better than Charlotte. Maybe I could convince Glenn he needed to work out of Wyoming for the summer. That way, we could escape the dreaded heat.

My phone rang so I set down my pad and reached for it inside my bag. I couldn't help but smile. "Look who it is," I said, chuckling as I answered the phone.

Andrea giggled. "I know, I know. I should've called you back ages ago."

"Yes, you should've, but I understand. You're a married woman now. How the hell are you?"

"Tired," she said with a sigh. "But the school year's almost up, so I'll have a nice long summer."

"Must be nice to have that kind of time off. Not that I'm complaining. The money is nice where I work."

"I'm sure it is," she replied slyly. "You happen to be working for one of the highest paid men in the country. I like telling the women at work I'm best friends with a celebrity."

I scoffed. "Please. I'm just an assistant who goes with him everywhere. Nobody knows who I am."

"But you said you don't do much for him, except write his proposals and follow him around. Most assistants answer the phone, get coffee, and all that other bullshit."

It was true. Glenn never had me do his errands. He had other people for that. "I don't know, Andy. The whole situation is strange, but I'm not gonna argue. I get to see the world and enjoy doing it. At least, I have time to write."

"True."

In the background, I heard Cliff's voice. "Put her on the speakerphone so I can say hey."

Andrea snickered. "Okay. Emma, you mind?"

"Not at all."

Cliff and Andrea were my best friends since college. I'd had others, but they either transferred or left without a trace.

She pressed the button and Cliff shouted. "Emma! What's up, babe?"

I couldn't help but laugh. "Sitting in Charleston, enjoying the weather. My boss has pretty much let me have the whole week off."

"Nice. Well, you need to come up here and visit, especially in another six months."

"Cliff!" Andrea scolded. "We were going to tell her together."

Excitement bubbled in my chest. I had a feeling I already knew what was going on. "What is it?" I asked happily.

"We're pregnant!" they called out at the same time.

"Aww . . . guys, that's awesome. Congratulations. I will definitely make it a priority to get up there. I can't wait to see my niece or nephew." Cliff and Andrea were like family. I was an only child, so being an honorary aunt was going to be exciting. I just hated that they moved all the way up to Maine. It wasn't like I could drive to see them anytime I wanted.

"We can't wait to see you," Andrea gushed. "I miss our late night talks. Plus, it'll be around Christmas when the baby's due. We can celebrate the holidays together."

"Yes, definitely. I can't wait."

We said our goodbyes and I hung up the phone. I missed my family and friends more than anything. Being able to travel was nice, but I was mostly alone.

"Emma," a deep, smooth voice called out.

Chills ran down my arms and my pulse spiked. I wasn't expecting to see him so soon. What was he doing out here? I turned and watched Wade Chandler walk toward me, dressed in a white button-down and gray pants.

"Mr. Chandler," I blurted, getting to my feet. Running my hands over my ponytail, I could feel the knots from where the wind blew my hair.

Wade climbed the stairs to the gazebo, his posture tall and straight. "You can call me Wade," he said. I nodded and smiled, hoping my nervousness didn't show through. "My father told me you were out here. I hope you don't mind."

He had dark hair like Glenn, but his eyes were a bright blue, whereas Glenn's were green. He had three other brothers, who all shared the same looks and build, but they didn't work for Chandler Enterprises.

"No, not at all. I see you got into town safely. Traffic wasn't bad, was it?" I asked, trying to make small talk. I hated silence in a conversation. If we were going to work together twenty-four-seven, we had to be able to talk to each other.

He leaned against the gazebo, his posture slowly relaxing. "There was a bit in Columbia, but nothing more than that."

"That's good."

His gaze landed on the notepad. "What are you working on?"

Shrugging, I felt the heat rise to my cheeks. "Songs. I dabble in song-writing when I have time. I figured since your dad hadn't needed me here recently, I'd give it a go again." I looked up at him and he actually smiled.

"That sounds interesting. I love a good song. What kind do you write?"

He was definitely winning points with me. Maybe he wouldn't be so bad to work for. "Mainly pop rock. I was in a band in college. Always thought we'd make it to the big time, but that didn't happen." Clearing my throat, I picked up the notebook. "I guess we should probably head back and get ready for dinner, huh? Your father said there's someone else joining us tonight?"

Wade nodded. "A friend of the family. Why don't I walk you back and we can talk on the way?"

"Sounds good."

Wade's arm brushed against mine as we made our way across the street. "My father tells me he brought up the idea of you working for me when he hands the company over."

I nodded. "He did."

"Is that something you'd be interested in?"

"Of course." I made eye contact. "I said as much to your father."

"Yes, I know. But I wanted to hear it from you," he stated, keeping his eyes on mine. We stopped on the sidewalk and I faced him.

"Did you not believe him?" I asked with a laugh.

His gaze narrowed as if he was trying to figure me out. "I didn't think you'd agree to it. My father and I are two different men, Emma. Things might be a little more complicated working for me."

"You have nothing to worry about, as far as I'm concerned. I can handle a challenge."

His lip tilted up slightly in an amused smile. "I look forward to seeing you in action. How about we grab some drinks after dinner? It'll give us a chance to get to know each other."

"Okay," I agreed with a nod. "But I must warn you . . . there's nothing exciting to learn about me."

We crossed the street to Glenn's house and he opened the front gate. "For some reason, I don't believe that's true. There's more to you than you think."

#

I slipped on my brand new, silky blue dress and checked my hair and makeup in the mirror. Normally, I wouldn't care about the way I looked so much, but I had to keep up appearances since I was employed by the Chandler's. They wouldn't exactly want me parading around in yoga pants like I did before I started working for them.

Opening my bedroom door, I could already smell the meal Mrs. Walker was making. Hopefully, I wouldn't spill food on my dress and look like an idiot. I had a habit of dropping food on my clothes. Cliff and Andrea used to laugh at me all the time when we'd go out because I'd always have to make a trip back to the dorms to change.

When I got downstairs to the dining room, Glenn and Wade were already there, speaking to each other in hushed tones by the large window. There were shiny plates on the table, with all sorts of silverware around them. Start from the outside and work your way in, was what I was told when it came to using the various forks and spoons. Give me just one of each and I'd be happy.

It wasn't long before Glenn noticed me at the door and the conversation ceased. "Emma, you look lovely tonight," he announced.

I smiled. "Thank you."

He beckoned me over to the table and Wade held out a seat for me. I sat down and he took the one on the right, while Glenn sat on my left at the head of the table. There was only one other place setting and it was across from me.

"Wine?" Glenn asked, holding up the bottle.

I nodded. "Sure."

He poured me a glass and I took a sip. It tasted like heaven, all fruity and crisp. It was so good I had to take another sip, and another, while we waited on the special guest. Not even a minute later, the dining room door opened and a man walked in. Only, he wasn't just anyone.

It'd been eight years and he'd surely changed, but there was no mistaking those gray eyes. His hair was the same light brown, and mussed up like all the guys did their hair these days. However, his body looked totally different. His cream colored, long-sleeve sweater hugged a set of muscular arms, and his face was more rugged, covered in a five o'clock shadow.

I almost choked on my wine. "Oh my God." Is it really him?

"Emma, are you okay?" Wade asked, his voice low.

"Yeah," I whispered. "I'm fine."

I waited for Preston to look at the table, and when his gaze finally caught mine, he paused for a slight second. In his face, I could see the friend I lost so long ago, but it vanished quickly.

Glenn and Wade both stood when Preston approached, and I shot up out of my seat, bumping the table with my jerky movements. Glenn grinned at me and then at Preston. "Preston Hale, I'd like you to meet Emma Turner. She's my assistant. Emma, this is Preston Hale, a close family friend. His father is one of my dearest friends."

Preston held out his hand and looked at me as if he'd never laid eyes on me before. "It's nice to meet you."

Was he being serious? I shook his hand and made sure to put a little extra squeeze in there for good measure. "Meet me? Surely, you remember who I am."

Glenn's eyes went wide. "Wait. You two already know each other?"

I nodded. "From college." I was about to add before he up and left without a trace, but thought better of it.

Glenn chuckled and smacked a hand on Preston's shoulder. "Well, isn't this a small world? You'll have to tell me some stories on this one." He nodded my way.

Preston's jaw clenched. "Can't. Don't remember her."

My mouth dropped open; it was like being punched in the gut and slapped in the face, all at the same time. No words would come out, so I sat there with a lump in my throat. In college, he'd been a close friend. I sang with him in his band, Silent Break. We connected on stage in a way I'd never felt with anyone. I cared about him, and had even been ready to take the next step in our relationship right before he up and disappeared. I never got to tell him how I felt. Now he looked at me as if I was a stranger.

The room fell silent. I wanted to say something, but I bit my tongue. It was going to be the longest dinner of my life.

#

Glenn and Wade spent most of the dinner talking, while Preston joined in with a few grunts here and there. What the hell happened to him? He wasn't the same twenty-year-old who liked to smile and have fun. Granted, he was never the happy-go-lucky type, but he was at least friendly. There were many nights where we stayed up late and talked about anything and everything. That was the guy I missed.

Once dinner was finished, Preston left the table, disappearing through the patio doors and onto the back porch. "Emma, you all right?" Glenn asked.

I plastered on a fake smile. "Of course. Why wouldn't I be?"

His gaze narrowed. "Come now, I know you better than that. It's obvious Preston's presence made you uncomfortable."

I snorted. "I guess I thought he'd remember me. We used to be good friends. I'm just baffled at this point."

Taking a sip of his whiskey, he stared at me over the rim of the glass. "Why don't you go out and talk to him?"

I glanced over at Wade and he nodded toward the patio door. We were supposed to grab drinks together. "Go. I'll come get you in a few minutes," he said.

Taking a deep breath, I slid out of my chair and walked to the patio doors. It was dark outside, so I couldn't see anything because of the lights inside the dining room. I opened the door and shut it behind me, the wind making my dress flutter. Preston wasn't on the deck, and I couldn't hear him anywhere.

Pulling out my phone, I texted Andrea.

Emma: You will not believe who showed up in Charleston. Preston Hale.

Emma: Get this, the asshole says he doesn't remember me.

Andrea: Oh wow! Where's he been? You sure he's not joking?

Emma: Nope. I don't know where he's been. He's changed.

Andrea: What the hell? That's insane.

Frustrated, I sat down on the wooden swing and huffed. "Fucking prick."

"Been called worse," Preston announced, appearing around the side of the house.

I shot up out of the swing and gasped. "Jesus, you scared the piss out of me."

There was no smile on his face as he climbed the stairs to the patio. "Sorry." Instead of stopping, he went straight toward the door, turning his back on me.

My blood boiled. "Really? That's how you're going to play this, after all these years? No, 'Hey, how ya been?' I—I can't believe this shit."

He paused and glanced at me over his shoulder, his expression unreadable.

"Why are you doing this? I was worried about you. You disappeared from our lives." For the longest time, I'd wondered if he was dead. He'd left no trace, no reason for leaving.

He looked like he was about to speak, but then Wade opened the patio door, nodding at Preston before settling his gaze on mine. "Ready to go?" he asked.

I glared at Preston, waiting on him to say anything, but I was met with silence. "Yep. I could use a drink about now." Storming past him, I didn't attempt to look back. If he didn't want to remember me, then so be it. Maybe it was time I forgot about him.

6

What the fuck of all fucks was Emma Turner doing with the Chandlers? I didn't think my time in Charleston could get any worse, but I was wrong. She was a distraction; one I didn't need. I watched how Wade was with her when they got back to the house after their night of drinks. He was too close. I tried to ignore the burning in my gut, but it was there. It was a feeling I hadn't had in a long time.

All I had to do was keep up the charade until I could get the hell out of town. The sun started to come up so I got out of bed and made coffee. I was too on edge to sleep. As soon as I sat down at the kitchen table, I glanced out the glass door and watched Glenn march over.

The door to the pool house opened and he charged in, his face a stony mask. "You're letting your anger get the better of you." He slammed the newspaper on the table. I didn't have to look at the headline to know what he was referring to. "You can't be doing this shit. It's sloppy. Make the kill and get out. No more, no less."

Now that Jim Butler was dead, the authorities were going straight to the people who hated him. The police were investigating Milly's mother, but I knew for a fact they weren't going to do anything about it. It was so the world would think they were doing something, when actually, they didn't give a fuck. Butler wasn't worth the time.

I drank the last of my coffee and looked at him. "The bastard deserved to feel pain. I couldn't give him the mercy of a quick kill."

Glenn's jaw clenched. "But you run the risk of exposing us. What if you were caught? My head would be on the chopping block if I let you screw this up."

"That's not gonna happen. I'm good at what I do."

He scoffed. "That's what's scary. You're worse than Wade. At least he's smart enough to enjoy life while he has it. You need to take some time for yourself."

I threw my hands in the air. "To do what exactly? Play golf? Relax by the pool? That shit's useless to me. There's too much that needs to get done."

"There are others in the team," he snapped. "They're all working on the list. No matter how many criminals you kill, there will always be more. You're not gonna get them all."

Fire burned in my stomach. "I can try."

Sighing, he took a seat at the table. "I didn't want to do this, but you're leaving me no choice. Starting today, you're done until I give you permission. I have other projects that'll keep you busy in the meantime."

Heart racing, I slammed my hand down on the table. "You can't stop me, Glenn. I have to do this." It was an addiction. If I stopped, there was no telling what I'd do.

He stared down at me. "I can try," he said, throwing my words back at me before storming to the door.

My whole body shook with rage. I wasn't going to let him deter me.

Stopping in his tracks, he faced me again. "Wade's in the basement working out. You might want to join him. He'll tell you what you need to know. Right now, I'm going to visit your father. Might want to consider going with me before we head back to Charlotte."

He left before I could get the final word in, just like Emma had done to me the night before. Rummaging through my bag, I grabbed a pair of gym shorts and changed. A few jabs at the punching bag was exactly what I needed.

Walking through the main house to get to the basement, I opened the back patio door and Emma was right there. She walked past me without a single word. Good. If she was pissed at me, it made my life a hell of a lot easier. I found the door to the basement and walked down the stairs to an open room filled with top of the line exercising equipment.

Wade was on the bench lifting weights, but he noticed me through the reflection in the mirror that lined the back wall. "Ready to get to work, Hale?"

"Depends. What do you mean by work?" I marched over to the punching bag and pounded away.

Wade set his weights down and walked over, grasping the punching bag while I hit it. My knuckles were on fire, but I kept going. I wanted to feel the pain; it let me know I wasn't completely numb.

"My father needs your help this week. Chandler Enterprises is expanding into a new industry and we need your help. Apparently, you have experience in this line of work."

Brows furrowed, I stopped and stared at him. "What the hell are you talking about?"

A mischievous leer spread across his face. "You're going into the music business, brother. Found out you had a band back in college." For fuck's sake. "We could use your help with finding some musicians here in Charleston. That is, if you don't want to audition yourself."

Sweat pouring down my face, I angrily wiped it off. "You've got to be shitting me. Did Emma tell you?"

His brows lifted. “I thought you didn’t know her.”

“I don’t,” I growled, realizing my slip.

He sighed. “No, it wasn’t her. Although, we did have a nice evening. And don’t worry, your name never came up.”

“It’s not good business to sleep with your assistant,” I said through clenched teeth.

He let go of the punching bag and walked back over to the weight bench. “What Emma and I do is our own business.” Laying down on the bench, he looked over at me. “And for your information, it was your father who told us about the band. He thinks it’ll help you.”

“Whatever, Chandler.” I grabbed a towel from the rack before heading toward the stairs. “I don’t need help.”

If Preston was going to ignore me, the least I could do was pretend it didn't bother me. When he came up from the basement and walked through the kitchen, I busied myself on my phone until the back door opened and shut. Looking to make sure he was gone, I turned to Mrs. Walker. "Do you need any help with breakfast?"

She waved me off and laughed. "Sweetheart, no. I've been doing this for years. I can cook with my eyes closed. Thank you though."

"You're welcome. But I'm right here if you need me." I was going to miss her when we went back to Charlotte. Glenn employed different people everywhere we went. The newspaper was on the kitchen table and my stomach dropped when I saw yet another murder in the area. "Mrs. Walker, did you see this?"

She turned around, squinting from across the room to see the article. "I did. Crazy, isn't it? But that nasty man deserved to die after what he did to his stepdaughter. I doubt anyone's shedding a tear over him."

My stomach rolled while reading about the physical and emotional abuse he put his stepdaughter through. She would be seventeen right now, carrying around a burden she'd never be able to live without.

"What kind of person would do something like that?" I whispered, tears burning my eyes. Sliding the newspaper away, I couldn't stomach any more. Wade walked in, showered up and already dressed to perfection. "Good morning," I said.

He nodded once and gave me a small smile. Even though we went out for drinks, he never let on that he wanted something from me—keeping it professional. I liked that about him. At first, I was worried he'd try to come onto me. That wasn't the way I wanted to start working for him.

He poured himself a cup of coffee and joined me at the table, only he didn't sit down. "Good morning. I wanted to tell you I'm heading back to Charlotte today. When you return to the office, we'll start working together more."

"Sounds great. I look forward to it."

Mrs. Walker wrapped up an egg and bacon sandwich and handed it to him. "Be safe going home. You need to visit more. I miss you and your brothers."

He looked at her and his gaze softened. "I will. Tell Clayton I owe him a game of golf."

Mrs. Walker kissed his cheek. "Will do, sweetheart. You take care."

"You do the same." Then he glanced down at me. "See you back in Charlotte."

"Okay," I replied with a nod.

Once he was gone, I stood and grabbed a plate from the counter so I could load it with eggs, bacon, and toast. As soon as I sat down to take my first bite, Preston walked through the back door. I didn't dare look at him, so I kept my focus on my plate until he turned his back to me. He fixed a plate of food and started back toward the door, but then Glenn came in.

"Wait," he commanded, staring right at Preston.

The muscles in Preston's jaw ticked, but he turned around slowly. "Can I help you?"

"Yes, you can. Take a seat."

I'd never heard Glenn sound so demanding before. He looked angry and I hoped it wasn't because of me. Preston stood frozen in place, then huffed and stormed over to the table, setting down his plate with a loud clank.

"Did Wade tell you what you'll be doing today?" Glenn asked me. His gaze shifted to Preston when I shook my head, then came back to me. "I'm sure you remember talking about expanding Chandler Enterprises, right?"

"Of course. But you never told me what you were going to do," I said.

"You're right, I didn't. I wanted to make sure I had everything in place before I announced it." He nodded over at Preston. "This is where he comes into the picture." Preston's eyes widened, his expression appalled. "We're expanding into the music industry. And since this guy has experience in the art, I'm putting him in charge. There are five auditions today and I need you both to work together. See if any of them are good enough to receive representation."

And just like that, I lost my appetite. The blood rushed from my face and I probably looked like a ghost.

"Are we done here?" Preston snapped impatiently.

Glenn nodded once. "Yep. Be ready in an hour. George will drive you and Emma to the theater."

Grabbing his plate, Preston walked out the door and back to the pool house. Glenn watched him go, wearing a look of sadness I'd never seen before.

"Please don't make me work with him," I pleaded, trying to process what just happened. "I can get along with just about anybody, but not him. He's changed."

His brows furrowed. "What happened between you two? I'm just wondering why he'd say he doesn't know you when you say otherwise."

I shrugged. "I don't know. One day, our band is practicing new songs, and the next, he up and disappears. Do you know where he's been the past few years? I've tried looking him up, but always come up empty."

His focus was on the pool house. "That's because you won't find anything. He's had a hard life, Emma. I'm hoping he'll come around. All I ask is that you please do this for me."

I didn't want to, but I couldn't say no. "Okay," I gave in. "I'll get ready to go."

#

After I finished breakfast, I hurried to my room to change into a pair of dress pants and a pink, silky top. When I walked downstairs, Preston waited by the front door, dressed in dark jeans and a light blue, fitted T-shirt. Other than his shitty demeanor, he was still one of the sexiest men I'd ever met.

"I'm ready," I called out.

Preston's gaze scanned down my body, but then he opened the door and walked out. Clenching my teeth, I begrudgingly followed behind him. Glenn's driver, George, stood by the car. He reminded me of the older guy in Men in Black. George opened the car door and we both slid in, but I made sure to sit as far away from Preston as humanly possible.

Once on the way, I kept my focus on the road until my phone rang. I pulled it out of my purse and saw Andrea's name pop up on the screen. "Hey," I answered.

"Hey, you never called me. Tell me what's going on. What's Preston's deal?"

I glanced over at him but he didn't acknowledge me. "Do you mind if I call you back later? I'm on my way to listen to some bands play. My boss wants to dabble in the music industry."

"Oh my God, that's awesome. It's a shame you and Cliff never joined up with another band."

"I know," I said low. "But it is what it is." I often wondered what it'd be like to travel the world and sing. For a time, I thought it was possible. Preston was an amazing guitarist and singer.

"All right. Call me back when you get a chance."

We hung up and I slipped the phone back into my purse. "That was Andrea, by the way," I said, knowing he wouldn't look at me. "Not that you care, but Cliff and Andrea got married last year. They're expecting a baby."

"Good for them," he grumbled.

The man was impossible. "Did you fall and hit your head or something? Or were you always a super mega douche and I was too stupid to see it?" More like too in love with him. Back in college, I never let on that I had feelings for him. I'd tried to keep my distance, especially since he was always with someone else. The girls loved him.

His head turned and he stared at me, eyes cold. "I'm not here to hold hands and skip down memory lane. Let's just do what we gotta do and be done."

"Fine," I said, shifting to look out the window. I couldn't stand to look at him anymore.

We arrived at the local arts theater and I hurried out of the car, not even waiting on George to open the door. The building was ancient, and according to the history books, it was the first theater ever to hit the Americas. It had been renovated a few times, but nothing took away from the architecture. You could look at it and tell it was built a long time ago, a classic beauty. I couldn't wait to go inside.

There was a lady standing by the entrance and she waved when I walked up. "Hi, you must be Ms. Turner," she greeted, holding out her hand. "I'm Miranda. Mr. Chandler told me you'd be arriving with Mr. Hale."

Smiling, I shook her hand. "It's good to meet you."

Preston stopped by my side, and wasn't a complete dick, taking her outstretched hand.

"The bands are all ready for you," she explained. "I'm going to show you inside and then leave you to it."

"Great, thanks." I followed her inside and breathed in the smell of the theater. It was amazing to think our ancestors from hundreds of years ago might have been in the same building. That was what I loved about Charleston—the history. I'd been dying to take one of the ghost tours I'd heard so much about.

Miranda handed us a stack of papers that had each band's information on it. "I'll be in the back if you need me. The bands were told to play one song, unless you prefer to hear more."

"Thank you," I said. When she hurried toward the back of the theater and took a seat, I turned to Preston. "You could pretend to look somewhat interested," I growled low.

Not waiting on an answer, I marched to the front row and took a seat, while he chose to sit a couple spots away. Since it was his job to find the talent, I waited on him to acknowledge the band, but he didn't. Cocksucker.

"Good morning," I announced. "Please, begin when you're ready."

The lead singer looked back at his band and nodded before staring down at me. "We're First Sanity, and the song we're going to play is called Summer. It's one of our biggest hits."

The second the guitar played, I was sucked back to a time eight years before. It reminded me of what it was like to belong to a group. I could almost see myself up on stage with Preston and Cliff, auditioning for opportunities like this.

A smile lit up my face and I closed my eyes. I didn't realize how much I'd missed it.

#

Once we arrived back at Glenn's house, Preston went straight through the side gate, no doubt to hole up in the pool house. Glenn was in the living room with a tumbler full of whiskey.

"How did it go?" he asked, sounding hopeful.

I set my purse on the couch. "The bands were great. I just wish I had a little input from my partner."

His lips pursed. "He didn't help, did he?"

"Not at all. In fact, he was a downright ass, refusing to acknowledge the bands, or me for that matter. Please tell me I don't have to work with him anymore. I didn't sign on for this."

Sighing, he tossed back his liquor. "I know, but I need your help. Just give it another week."

"A week?" I gasped incredulously. I couldn't handle another day.

Glenn stared right into my eyes, his features morphing. There was something about Preston that made him a different man—a man steeped in grief. "Please, Emma. All I ask is that you work with him for another week. There are more bands scheduled to play for the next few days, and then again on Monday and Tuesday of next week. Once Wednesday comes, you can head back to Charlotte."

"I'm starting to think I should ask for double time having to put up with him. As a side note, he won't make it to next week if he keeps up with this attitude. I will kill him first."

A mischievous smile spread across his face. "You're more than welcome to smack him around a few times. You won't get fired if you do."

Now that made me laugh. "It's a serious possibility." But then I sighed in defeat. "All right, I'll stay. But it's not something I want to do."

"Thank you, Emma. Just take notes on the bands you like, and what you like about them. I trust your opinion."

That meant a lot coming from one of the most successful men in the country. "If you trust my opinion, why does Preston have to be there?"

His gaze shifted over to the window and out to the pool house. "I'm sorry, you'll have to trust me on this." He blew out a heavy breath and grabbed his suitcase from the floor.

"Are you leaving?" Surely, he wasn't going to leave me alone with Preston.

Glenn glanced down at his bag and then over at me. "I'm needed in Charlotte. I have no doubt you'll be okay here by yourself. Mrs. Walker will cook your meals and you're more than welcome to drive one of my cars."

Dread settled into the pit of my stomach. It was going to be one of the worst weeks of my life. "Now I really need that double time pay."

He chuckled. "It's already been applied."

Mouth gaping, I watched him walk out the front door. Well, damn . . . I should've asked for triple pay.

8

Grabbing my car keys the next morning, I opened the front door of the pool house and walked out, only to run into the one woman I wanted to avoid.

"Hey," she gasped, tucking a strand of blonde hair behind her ear. She was dressed in a white skirt and a light blue top.

Clenching my teeth, the last thing I needed was to look at her long, tanned legs. But dammit to hell, I couldn't stop. There'd been a time when I'd wanted those legs wrapped around my waist as I fucked her. "What do you want?" I snapped.

Her face immediately soured. "And here I was trying to be nice." Huffing, she nodded toward the front of the house. "It's time to go. We have more auditions to listen to."

I scoffed. "Correction. You have more auditions to listen to. I have other plans."

Throwing her hands in the air, she walked away. "Have it your way, douchebag. Works better for me anyway. Now I don't have to look at your face for the rest of the day."

The girl was going to fucking kill me. She walked off and there was no denying how unbelievably sexy she was. Her hips swayed back and forth, reminding me of how I hadn't had sex in weeks. I could use a good fuck, but I didn't have time. As soon as I did what I had to do, it was back to my computer to find my next target.

The drive to Isle of Palms wasn't backed up with traffic like it usually was in the summer. Once school was out, it'd be that way soon enough. I hated being there when it was packed with people. My old childhood home was off the main strip of the island, just a quarter mile down from where Shelly's body was found. We always had a lot more privacy than some of the other places. And in the end, it was one of the main reasons nobody came to my mother's rescue; she wasn't heard.

It'd been seven years since I'd last visited the place. My father couldn't bring himself to sell it, even though he never stepped foot back into it once the investigation was complete. We'd combed that place from top to bottom and never found anything. No clues as to who the killer was.

When I arrived at my house, you could tell it'd been neglected. The yellow siding was more like a light brown, and some of the shrubs had grown across the stairs leading up to the door. It was one of the smallest houses on the island, but we had the best stretch of coastline all to ourselves. We never worried about swarms of people taking up our beach.

I looked up at the house and released a shaky breath. I'd spent years trying to make up for the loss of my mother and sister, but nothing worked. They were gone, no matter how many people I killed.

Taking the wooden steps two at a time, I reached a small piece of yellow crime scene tape still stuck to the railing, and my gut clenched. Everything from that night flashed through my mind.

I remembered walking through the door and seeing my mother's lifeless body on the living room floor, her chocolate-colored hair matted down with dried blood. My father's screams still echoed in my ears as he rushed over to check on her. It was a sound I never wanted to hear again.

Searching through my keys, I found the one for the front door and opened it. The smell of dust hit me, but was overpowered by the stench of death. I knew it was my own mind playing tricks on me, but it didn't keep me from staring at the spot where my mother had died.

Walking around the room, there was a thick layer of dust on everything. Nothing had been moved. I looked out the window at the swimming pool and there was nothing in it but a couple feet of dirty water and sand. What I wanted to avoid seeing most was the spot on the beach where my sister had been found. Her death would always be a puzzle to me. The thought of what happened to her made me goddamned sick to my stomach.

Closing my eyes, I turned away from the window and stormed up the stairs. My parents' room was the same as it'd always been. And across the hall, Cameron's door was shut. I stared at it, trying to remember if I'd shut it last time I was there. My hands shook and I could feel the rage inside my chest, aching to let loose. The door handle was cold as I grasped it, a sinking feeling washing over me. Something wasn't right.

I opened the door slowly, my heart thundering in my chest. Once I looked in her room, I realized why I had that sinking feeling in my gut. "Fuck," I growled. Everything in her drawers and closet were thrown across the room, as if someone had been searching for something. "Son of a bitch."

Nothing in the house was turned upside down, except for her room. I didn't like that at all. Pulling out my phone, I called Glenn.

"Shouldn't you be at the auditions?" he asked.

"Fuck that. We have bigger problems."

"What is it? Is Emma okay?"

"Yeah, she's fine. I'm at my old house. Cameron's room is ransacked. I think someone was looking for something. Nothing else in the house was touched."

"What the hell? How did they break in?"

I rushed down the stairs to the back door and it was locked, sealed perfectly. What the fuck was going on? All of the windows were secure, and there was nothing that'd suggest a break in. "There's no evidence of tampering. The front door was locked and the same goes for the back door and all of the windows. Whoever it was must've had a key."

"Holy shit, this changes things, Preston. If the same killer is back in town and has a key to your house, then the murder was personal. We need to go back to the beginning." Which meant seeking out Cameron's close friends. "Just do me a favor and keep this under wraps. If the fucker finds we're onto him, he might run. With Shelly being found just a few short days ago, he's probably still around."

Rage consumed me. "Got it. I know what to do."

I had an hour before I needed to be at the theater, so I stopped at one of my new favorite cafés down the street. It had the best blueberry scones and hot chocolate. Once I got my order, I sat down at one of the small, white tables and blew the steam off my hot chocolate. I was glad I got in before the morning rush.

Reading the newspaper on the table beside me, I caught a headline about a woman's body being found on the beach. She'd been my age. And still no leads as to who the killer was. Scary. If anyone tried to hurt me, I'd fight until my last breath.

"Good morning, Ms. Turner," a voice called out.

Gasping, I jerked my head up, almost knocking over my hot chocolate. John laughed and steadied my cup before sitting down in front of me. He had sandy, blond hair shaved close to his head, and a wide smile, which I didn't see often on men. It was refreshing.

"Didn't mean to scare you. I saw you sitting here and thought I'd come over and say hey."

"Hey," I echoed, moving the newspaper out of the way. "How are you?"

John Tallman was the lead singer and guitarist for First Sanity, one of my top three choices from the auditions. Setting his coffee down, he smiled. "Doing good. Just getting ready to head into work. I like to stop here in the mornings to get my coffee."

"Work? I thought you played for a living?"

He shrugged. "It pays the bills, but it's not enough yet. The guys and I are hoping to change that one day. Right now, I work at the aquarium."

That was when I noticed the aquarium logo on his green polo shirt. "Sounds like fun. Do you get to feed the fish?"

Chuckling, he took a sip of his coffee. "That and clean the tanks."

"I'll have to stop by." I might as well. I didn't have anything else to do, since Preston basically left me on my own.

"I'll be happy to show you around. How long are you in town for?" he asked.

"Til next Wednesday, then I'm heading back to Charlotte. I have a few more bands to consider."

Clearing his throat, he glanced down at his coffee. "Have you and your partner made any decisions yet?"

I snorted. Preston had completely distanced himself the past two days. I kept trying to tell myself it didn't bother me, but it did. Especially when he'd leave late at night and not come back until dawn. I couldn't help but wonder where he went. "His opinion doesn't matter to me. I'll be making the decision on my own. But I can say that your band is one of my favorites. It reminds me of the one I used to be in many years ago."

His face lit up. "You were in a band?"

"Is it so hard to believe?" I laughed.

He shook his head. "Not at all. Did you play or sing?"

"Both," I confessed. "I play the keyboard. It was an amazing feeling being on stage."

"What happened? Why aren't you in one now?"

I thought back to that time and how heartbroken I was when Preston left. "The leader of our band left, and we never quite recovered."

His gaze softened. "I'm sorry to hear that. I don't know what I'd do if I didn't have my band."

"Just hold on to it for as long as you can."

"I plan on it." He looked down at his phone and sighed. "I should probably get going. Don't want to be late for work." His gaze shifted to my left, then back to me, before doing it again. When his brows furrowed, I turned and looked behind me. There was nothing there.

"Everything okay?" I asked.

"Do you have a boyfriend, or a husband?" His gaze shifted to my left hand.

"No, why?"

He nodded toward the door. "There was a guy outside who couldn't stop staring at you. He was over by the tree. But when he saw me notice him, he walked away."

I jerked my attention to the windows again. "Really? What did he look like?"

"Couldn't tell," he replied. "But he looked around our age."

"Was it my partner?"

He shrugged. "Don't know. I never paid much attention to him the other day."

Goose bumps flittered across my arms and up my neck. "That's strange. Maybe this guy thought he knew me."

"Don't know. Seemed kind of weird though," he said, getting to his feet. "Just be careful. Do you want me to walk you to your car?"

I took another bite of my scone and waved him off. "I'll be fine. Go, before you're late for work. I'll call you with my decision early next week."

He smiled again. "I look forward to it."

Once he was gone, I finished my scone and hot chocolate, keeping my gaze on the tree just outside the window. If Preston was following me, we were going to have some serious problems. I wasn't about to put up with it.

I looked down at my phone. There was still thirty minutes before I had to be at the theater. Making a split decision, I got up and headed home.

Preston's black sports car was in the driveway. Storming past the side gate, I circled around to the pool house. The blinds were open on all the windows, and I could see him walking around inside before sitting down with his back to me at the kitchen table. Instead of knocking, I slammed open the door.

Clearly knowing it was me, he didn't even bother turning around. "Can I help you?" he asked.

The man was seriously going to drive me insane. "Yeah, you can stop following me around."

"And why would I be doing that?"

"Hell if I know. You've been skulking around all hours of the night, so there's no telling. Maybe you get off on it. Who the fuck knows. But I'll let you know—right fucking now—I don't like being watched."

He jerked around, eyes blazing as he shot up out of the chair. "What do you mean being watched?"

His reaction wasn't what I expected. Instead of anger, like I'd seen for days, there was concern in his gray eyes. Holding up my hands, I backed away. It was best to just stay away from him. "I don't have time to deal with this shit right now. Consider yourself warned." Turning on my heel, I hurried off.

"Emma!" he shouted after me, but I couldn't be bothered to stop.

If it wasn't him watching me . . . then who was it?

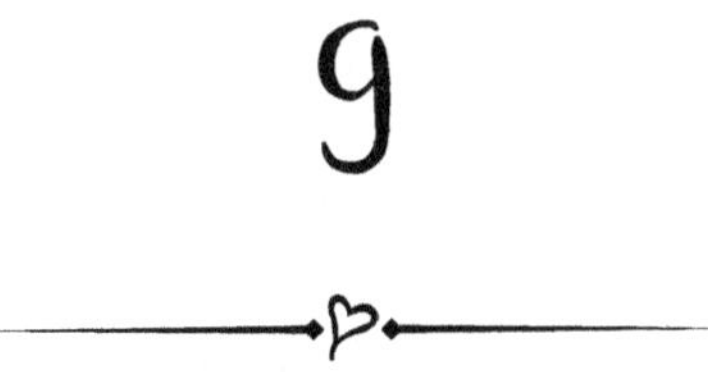

It was nine o'clock and I knew she wouldn't be done at the theater until two. I had plenty of time to do what I needed to do and then meet her there to make sure she got back okay. She wasn't going to like it, but I didn't give a shit. The only person who could follow her around was me . . . and it hadn't been me earlier this morning.

After searching for my sister's best friend, Lainey McGee, on the internet, I found all of her information. She was now an accountant in Mt. Pleasant, only a short drive away, and married to a Dillon Walsh.

Picking up my phone, I called her office. I hadn't seen her since I left home for college.

"Hello, Lainey Walsh," she answered.

I closed my eyes, clenching my teeth hard. "Lainey, it's Preston, Cameron's brother." She gasped and the line went quiet. "I need to talk to you."

"Jesus Christ, Preston. I haven't seen or heard about you in years. How are you?"

"Not good." There was no reason to lie. "We need to talk. I have some questions I need to ask you."

"O-okay," she stuttered uneasily. "I'm here until three. If you want, you can come here."

"Be there in twenty." I hung up and got in my car.

It didn't take long to get there, and when I arrived, she was outside by her car. The short, red hair she'd had before was now long, and she was pregnant. Years back, I remembered listening to her and Cameron talk about how they were going to get married at the same time and have kids together. It was what they'd planned all their lives.

Lainey's eyes went wide when she saw me get out of my car. She slapped a hand to her mouth and walked toward me, her arms outstretched. "It's so good to see you," she cried, trying to hug me. Her stomach got in the way, so it ended up being more of a pat on the shoulders.

She wiped tears from under her eyes. "How's your dad doing?" she asked.

I shrugged, not interested in talking about my father. "Don't know. Just got into town. I need to ask you some questions about Cameron though." Her lips trembled and she rubbed her stomach like she was in pain. Great. The last thing I needed was for her to have her baby because I stressed her out. "Are you okay?"

She blew out a shaky breath and nodded. "I'm fine. Been having contractions. What all do you want to know?" Her watery gaze looked up at me.

"Do you know if Cameron ever gave anyone a key to our house?"

With pursed lips, she shook her head. "Not that I know of. Unless she gave one to Adam. Why do you ask?" Adam Payne had been Cameron's boyfriend of five years, up until she was killed. She grabbed my arm. "You don't think he did something, do you?"

Adam had been playing in a football game at Duke the night she was killed. He was never even a suspect. "No," I answered truthfully. "Someone broke into the house recently, and ransacked Cameron's room. They had to have gotten in by key."

She slapped a hand over her mouth. "Oh no. What were they looking for?"

"I don't know, but I was hoping you'd have some ideas. Do you know if Cam hid anything in her room? Like secret things she didn't want anyone to find?"

Lainey shrugged. "We all did stuff like that. I know she had a diary. Where she kept it, I have no clue."

If she had a diary, all I had to do was find it. In order to do that, I had to go back. "Thanks, Lainey. I'm sorry I had to come to you like this."

Her lips trembled as she smiled. "It was good to see you, Preston. You and Cameron have the same eyes. It's like I can see her in them."

Chest tightening, I turned on my heel. "Take care of yourself, Lainey. Congrats on the baby."

"I'm naming her Cameron," she called out. I paused and glanced over my shoulder. Lainey rubbed her stomach and smiled at me.

"Cam would've liked that," was all I could say. I had to get out of there. Hopping in my car, I sped away, hands shaking. The pain triggered the need to kill. Eventually, I'd find the fucker who murdered my sister and mother, but until then, I had to do what needed to be done.

Once I was back at the pool house, I ripped open my laptop and logged onto the list. There were countless targets all over the fucking country. Until the day I died, I would go after them. It just so happened there was a target a couple hours away, in Myrtle Beach.

But first, I had to make sure Emma was safe.

#

She walked out of the theater at two o'clock, with a smile on her face. She loved music. I knew it from the very beginning, back when I first met her in college. It was why I agreed to let her sing with me.

Her smile disappeared the second she saw me standing by her car. "What are you doing here?" Her face turned red, nostrils flaring. She was sexy as hell when she was pissed.

I blocked her from getting into her car. "I wanted to make sure you got back to Glenn's safely."

She scoffed. "Why do you care? Get out of my way."

"I'm not going anywhere until you listen to me," I said, standing firm. I looked into her bright green eyes, something I'd tried to avoid since being around her. Once I had her attention, I continued, "It wasn't me who was watching you earlier."

Her face paled and she froze. "If it wasn't you, then who was it?"

"I don't know, but it's best you not wander around the city alone."

She snorted. "Please, Mary Poppins, I've done just fine on my own for years. It's not like I need a nanny, I know how to take care of myself. Besides, aren't you the one who left me alone the last few days?"

Narrowing my gaze, I crossed my arms over my chest. "It was a mistake. It won't happen again."

Her scowl turned into a leer and she laughed, but I could see the pain in her eyes. "Don't you get it? I don't want you around. I'm just here to do my job until next Wednesday, when I can go home, and hopefully never see you again." We stared at each other for the longest time, but she broke contact first. "Can you please move out of the way? I'd like to get back."

Knowing she was about to break down, I stepped out of the way so she could get in the car. "I'll follow you home."

Glenn's car roared to life and she sped away before I could get back in mine. It wasn't hard to keep up with her, and when we arrived, she bolted inside. I followed behind her, giving her the distance she needed. It didn't surprise me when she slammed the door to her bedroom.

"My goodness," Mrs. Walker called out, hurrying from the kitchen. She looked at me, then up the stairs. "Is everything okay?"

I shrugged. "I'm used to people being pissed at me."

She grinned. "Something tells me you bring it on yourself. Don't worry, she'll get over it. I've seen the way she looks at you."

"With what, disgust?"

"No." She chuckled with a wave of her hand. "She cares about you. But I have to say, you're going about it all wrong."

"Trust me, it's for the best."

"Suit yourself." She turned to head back into the kitchen, her voice echoing down the hall. "If you were my husband, I'd have beaten you silly by now." I'd have done a lot worse than that if I was Emma. "Do you want me to bring your dinner out to the pool house?"

I sat down on the couch and flipped the TV on. "Nah, I'll be eating in here tonight." I needed to make sure Emma was safe in bed, before I left.

Printed by Libri Plureos GmbH in Hamburg,
Germany